GEORGE WASHINGTON CARVER
PLANT DOCTOR

First Steck-Vaughn Edition 1992

Copyright © 1989 American Teacher Publications

Published by Steck-Vaughn Company

Library of Congress number: 89-3837

Library of Congress Cataloging in Publication Data.

Benitez, Mirna.
 George Washington Carver, plant doctor/Mirna Benitez; illustrated by Meryl Henderson.

 (Real readers)
 Summary: A biography of the agriculturist for beginning readers, chronicling his struggle to get an education, his work at the Tuskegee Institute, and how he helped popularize peanuts as a cash crop in the South.
 1. Carver, George Washington, 1864?–1943—Juvenile literature. 2. Afro-American agriculturists—Biography—Juvenile literature. 3. Agriculturists—United States—Biography—Juvenile literature. 4. Peanuts—Juvenile literature. [1. Carver, George Washington, 1864?–1943. 2. Agriculturists. 3. Afro-Americans—Biography.] I. Henderson, Meryl, ill. II. Title. III. Series.
 S417.C3B46   1989   630′.92′4—dc19 [B] [92]   89-3837

ISBN 0-8172-3522-1   hardcover library binding

ISBN 0-8114-6719-8   softcover binding

    4 5 6 7 8 9 0   96 95 94 93 92

George Washington CARVER
Plant Doctor

by Mirna Benitez

illustrated by
Meryl Henderson

STECK-VAUGHN
C O M P A N Y
A Subsidiary of National Education Corporation

Do you like to eat peanuts? Did you know that peanuts are used in many things?

Today, lots of people like to eat peanuts. And lots of things are made with peanuts. But 100 years ago, people did not eat or use many peanuts. Then a man named Dr. George Washington Carver showed people that peanuts are good for many, many things.

Who was George Washington Carver?

George Washington Carver was a scientist who worked with plants. George worked with plants from the time he was a little boy in the 1860s. He gave his plants water, sun, and shade. He raked and weeded.

Farmers would ask George to look at sick plants. George would find ways to make the plants well. George was so good with plants that people called him the "Plant Doctor."

To get to be a real plant doctor, George had to go to school. But that was not easy for George to do. At the time he was a little boy, some schools did not take black students. The school where George lived would not let him in.

So, George had to leave home to go to school. He had to leave Susan and Moses Carver. Susan and Moses were not George's mother and father, but they treated him like a son. George's real mother had been the Carvers' slave. After she died, George lived with them.

George went off to school when he was 12. He missed the Carvers, but he liked going to school. He learned fast. When he learned all he could, he made his way to a new school. To keep on learning, George made his way from school to school for a long, long time.

George made new friends to live with in each new place he went. He helped them with jobs like washing and cleaning. He helped all his new friends grow plants.

Years and years passed. George had learned enough and saved enough to go to college. He was going to be a real plant doctor at last!

George was happy at college. He learned to paint. He learned to sing. And he learned all he could about plants. He did experiments to find out new things about plants.

Soon he was a real plant doctor. He was asked to give classes at the college in Ames, Iowa. Many people came to know of Dr. George Washington Carver and his work with plants.

One man who came to know of George's work was Booker T. Washington. Mr. Washington ran a college for black students. This college was in a place called Tuskegee, Alabama.

Mr. Washington wrote to George. "Our college needs a scientist to help the students learn about plants. You are the best plant doctor we know. Will you come to Tuskegee to help?"

In 1896, George packed his bags. He filled them with seeds and books about plants. He was sad to leave Ames, but he wanted to help at Tuskegee. He wanted to help black students learn.

Tuskegee surprised George. George was used to a college with a fine lab and many books. But Tuskegee was a new college. It did not have lots of things. It did not have a science lab. George had to make a lab with old cups, plates, pots, and pans. He and his students needed a place to work with plants!

George did not work just with students. He worked with farmers, too. At that time, farmers in Alabama needed lots of help. The cotton they planted was not growing well. The farmers had nothing to sell.

George knew why the cotton was not doing well. First, a little bug called the boll weevil liked to eat the cotton plants. And the cotton plants that were left could not get something called nitrogen that they needed to grow well.

All plants need nitrogen to grow well. Plants get nitrogen from the soil they grow in. Some plants take nitrogen from the soil and then put it back. Other plants take nitrogen from the soil but do not put it back.

Cotton plants take nitrogen from the soil but do not put it back. Farmers in the South had been planting cotton for 300 years. Each year, the plants used up more and more nitrogen. Now there was not enough nitrogen left in the soil for new cotton plants to grow well.

George had a way to help the farmers.
He wanted them to plant peanuts. Boll
weevils do not eat peanuts. And peanuts
are plants that put nitrogen back into
the soil after using it.

Many farmers did what George said.
When they planted peanuts, they had
big crops. Boll weevils did not eat the
peanuts. And the peanuts put nitrogen
back into the soil. Then when the farmers
planted cotton another year, the cotton
had enough nitrogen to grow well.

Then one day a farmer came to see George. "I planted peanuts," she said. "I want to sell them, but no one wants peanuts! How will I use all of the peanuts? What will I sell?"

At first George did not know what to do. When he had asked farmers to plant peanuts, he did not think about selling them! George knew he had to help!

Then George went to his lab. He did not step outside for weeks and weeks. He mixed and mashed. He did many experiments. He was looking for new ways to use peanuts.

At last George came out of his lab. He had worked for a long time, but he was happy. In the weeks he had worked, he had made lots of things with peanuts.

George used peanuts to make ink, cream, coffee, foods, and many more things. He made more than 300 things, all from peanuts.

Dr. George Washington Carver helped farmers all of his life. He learned many new things about plants that still help people today. He was a plant doctor who helped people, too.

Sharing the Joy of Reading

Beginning readers enjoy reading books on their own. Reading a book is a worthwhile activity in and of itself for a young reader. However, a child's reading can be even more rewarding if it is shared. This sharing can enhance your child's appreciation — both of the book and of his or her own abilities.

Now that your child has read **George Washington Carver: Plant Doctor**, you can help extend your child's reading experience by encouraging him or her to:

- Retell the story or key concepts presented in this story in his or her own words. The retelling can be oral or written.

- Create a picture of a favorite character, event, or concept from this book.

- Express his or her own ideas and feelings about the subject of this book and other things he or she might want to know about this subject.

Here is an activity that you can do together to help extend your child's appreciation of this book: You and your child can grow a peanut plant of your own. Take two or three unroasted peanuts still in their shells. Wet paper towels and place in a jar. Put the peanuts on top of the paper towels, then close the lid, and let sit. When the peanuts have sprouted, plant them in a pot, and water them. You and your child can watch the growth of your peanut plant.

Community Helpers at Work

A Day in the Life of a
Police Officer

by Heather Adamson

Consultant:
Jeffrey B. Bumgarner, Ph.D.
Department of Political Science and Law Enforcement
Minnesota State University, Mankato

Capstone
press

Mankato, Minnesota

First Facts is published by Capstone Press,
1710 Roe Crest Drive, North Mankato, Minnesota 56003
www.capstonepub.com

Library of Congress Cataloging-in-Publication Data
Adamson, Heather, 1974—
    A day in the life of a police officer / by Heather Adamson.
    p. cm.— (First facts. Community helpers at work)
    Includes bibliographical references and index.
    Contents: What do police officers wear during their shifts?—What happens at a
briefing?—What do police officers drive?—How do police officers know where help is
needed?—How do police officers help in emergencies?—What do police officers do when
they are not stopping crime?—How do police officers know if someone is speeding?—
What happens at the end of a shift?
        ISBN-13: 978-0-7368-2285-5 (library binding)   ISBN-10: 0-7368-2285-2 (library binding)
        ISBN-13: 978-0-7368-4670-7 (softcover pbk.)   ISBN-10: 0-7368-4670-0 (softcover pbk.)
1. Police—Juvenile literature. 2. Police patrol—Juvenile literature. [1. Police. 2. Police
patrol. 3. Occupations.] I. Title. II. Series.
    HV7922.A33 2004
    363.2—dc21   2003000152

Credits
Jennifer Schonborn, designer; Jim Foell, photographer; Eric Kudalis,
  product planning editor

Artistic Effects
Ingram Publishing, PhotoDisc

Capstone Press wishes to thank Officer David Queen and the Minneapolis Police Department
  for their help in the photographing of this book.

Table of Contents

What do police officers wear during their shifts? 4

What happens at a briefing? 7

What do police officers drive? 8

How do police officers know where help
is needed? 11

How do police officers help in emergencies? 12

What do police officers do when
they are not stopping crime? 14

How do police officers know if
someone is speeding? 16

What happens at the end of a shift? 18

Amazing But True! 20

Equipment Photo Diagram 20

Glossary 22

Read More 23

Internet Sites 23

Index 24

What do police officers wear during their shifts?

Police officers wear uniforms with badges. Uniforms help people notice officers who are working. Officer David wears a bulletproof vest under his shirt. He carries handcuffs, a gun, and a baton on his belt. His belt also holds a two-way radio to contact the station.

Fun Fact:
More than 441,000 people work as city police officers in the United States.

6:00 in the
morning

7:00 in the morning

What happens at a briefing?

Officers meet with the sergeant for a briefing at the start of each shift. The sergeant explains any crimes that happened during the last shift. The sergeant also tells the officers their duties. Officer David and Officer Melissa will work together on patrol.

What do police officers drive?

Police officers use many kinds of vehicles to patrol. They sometimes use bikes or horses.

9:30 in the morning

David drives a patrol car. The car has lights, a siren, a radio, a camera, and a computer. Officer David drives around watching for crime. He looks for anyone who needs help.

12:00 in the
afternoon

How do police officers know where help is needed?

Dispatchers answer 911 phone calls and tell police officers where to go. While David and Melissa are eating lunch, the dispatcher's voice comes over the radio. It says, "10-52." This means there is a car crash with injuries. David and Melissa rush to the scene a few blocks away.

How do police officers help in emergencies?

Police officers are trained to work quickly in an emergency. David directs traffic safely around the crash. Melissa uses the radio to call an ambulance and a tow truck. She gives first aid to the driver.

 Fun Fact:
The United States has more than 12,600 city police departments and 3,070 sheriffs' departments.

12:30 in the afternoon

13

What do police officers do when they are not stopping crime?

Police officers help their communities. They want people to be safe and healthy. Today, David and Melissa tell kids about the dangers of drugs. Flash, a police dog, comes along to show how he can sniff out drugs.

 Fun Fact:
New Jersey was the first state to have bulletproof vests for all its police dogs.

2:00 in the
afternoon

15

How do police officers know if someone is speeding?

Police officers use radar guns to check vehicle speeds. An alarm on the radar gun sounds. A driver did not slow down for the school zone. David flashes the patrol car's lights. The driver stops. David gives the driver a ticket. He explains that school zones keep kids safe.

17

What happens at the end of a shift?

Police officers return to the station at the end of their shifts. Officer David returns the patrol car and keys. He fills out reports at his desk. David greets the officers who are coming on duty. It is time for him to go home.

4:00 in the
afternoon

19

Amazing But True!

The first radios for police cars were made in 1928. The police station could send radio messages to police cars. Officers could only listen. Now police use two-way radios so officers can talk to the station as well.

Lights

Doors
back doors only open from the outside

Cap

Badge

Radio

Gun

Flashlight

Keys

Gloves

21

Glossary

ambulance (AM-byuh-luhnss)—a vehicle that takes sick or hurt people to a hospital

baton (buh-TON)—a small bat officers use to stop criminals from fighting; officers are trained to block punches and knock back criminals safely with their batons.

dispatcher (diss-PACH-ur)—a person who answers 911 calls and assigns rescue workers

patrol (puh-TROLE)—to watch a certain area by walking or riding by it often

radar (RAY-dar)—a machine that uses radio waves to locate objects; police officers use radar guns to measure how fast a vehicle travels.

sergeant (SAR-juhnt)—officer in charge of other patrol officers

shift (SHIFT)—a set amount of time to work

Read More

Englart, Mindi Rose. *Police Officer.* How Do I Become A. San Diego: Blackbirch Press, 2003.

Kottke, Jan. *A Day with Police Officers.* Hard Work. New York: Children's Press, 2000.

Rubinstein, Jonathan. *On the Job with a Police Officer, Protector of the Peace.* On the Job with Bridgit & Hugo. Hauppauge, N.Y.: Barron's, 2001.

Internet Sites

Do you want to find out more about police officers?
Let FactHound, our fact-finding hound dog,
do the research for you!

Here's how:
1. Visit *http://www.facthound.com*
2. Type in the **Book ID** number:
   0736822852
3. Click on **FETCH IT**.

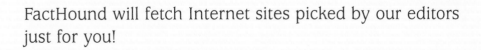

FactHound will fetch Internet sites picked by our editors just for you!

Index

alarm, 17
ambulance, 12

baton, 4
belt, 4
bike, 8
briefing, 7

crime, 7, 9

desk, 18
dispatcher, 11
drugs, 14
duty, 18

handcuffs, 4
horses, 8

keys, 18

lights, 9, 17

patrol, 7, 8, 9, 17, 18

radar gun, 17
radio, 4, 9, 11, 12, 20
reports, 18

school zone, 17
sergeant, 7
shift, 7, 18
siren, 9
station, 4, 18, 20

ticket, 17
tow truck, 12
traffic, 12

uniforms, 4

vest, 4